Dad!
I can't sleep

A Red Fox Book

Published by Random House Children's Books
20 Vauxhall Bridge Road, London SW1V 2SA

A division of The Random House Group Ltd
London Melbourne Sydney Auckland
Johannesburg and agencies throughout the world

5 7 9 10 8 6

First Published in Great Britain by Andersen Press Ltd 1994

Red Fox edition 1996

Printed in Hong Kong

The Random House Group Limited Reg. No. 954009

ISBN 0 09 961071 X

Dad!
I can't sleep

Written and illustrated by
Michael Foreman

RED FOX

Little Panda couldn't sleep.
"Mum!" he called. "Can I have a drink?"

Mum said, "It's your turn, Dad. I've done enough today."

Dad took Little Panda a drink, kissed him goodnight and went downstairs.

"Dad!" called Little Panda. "I still can't sleep. Can I
have another drink?"
"No," said Dad. "Go to sleep."
"I can't," said Little Panda.
"Count sheep," said Dad. "Then you'll go to sleep."
"How?" said Little Panda.

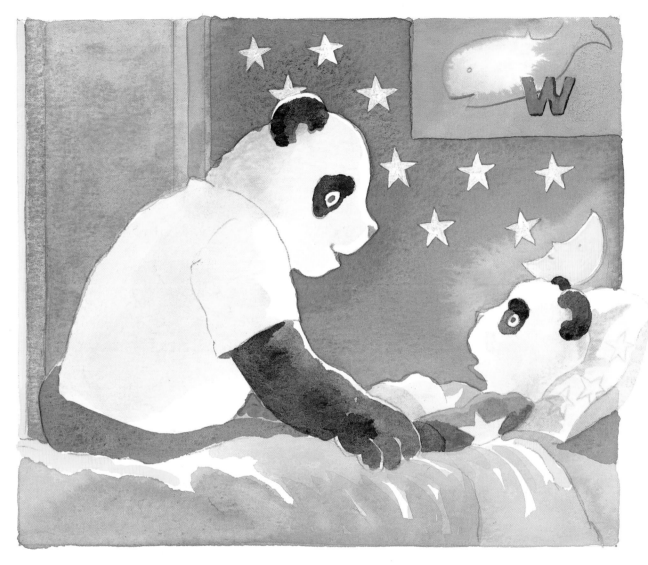

Dad climbed the stairs and sat on Little Panda's bed.
"How do I count sheep, Dad?" asked Little Panda.
"Just close your eyes," said Dad. "Now imagine sheep
jumping over a fence. Count them as they jump. One.
Two. Three. Four. Five. Six. Then you will fall asleep."

Little Panda closed his eyes and counted sheep.
"One. Two. Three. Four. Five and a lamb.
Six. Seven and another lamb..."
Quietly, Dad went downstairs.

"Dad!" called Little Panda.
"I can't sleep."
"Count sheep!" called Dad.

"I've done that and I still can't sleep," called Little Panda.
"Count something else," shouted Dad.
"Count cows!"

Little Panda closed his eyes and
counted cows.
"One. Two. Three. Four. Five. Six.
Seven. Eight. Nine.
Dad! I still can't sleep."

"I am not coming up again!" shouted Dad.
"Count pigs or tigers!"
Little Panda counted tigers.
"Sixteen. Seventeen. Eighteen. Nineteen
tigers and three little pigs."

"Dad! I still can't sleep."
"Count elephants! And I
don't want to hear from
you again," shouted Dad.
Little Panda counted
elephants.
"Forty-six. Forty-seven.
Forty-eight. Forty-nine."

Then he counted
rhinos and hippos,
giraffes and polar bears
and still he couldn't sleep.
"Dad! I've counted all sorts o
things and I still can't sleep."

"Dinosaurs!" shouted Dad.
"Have you counted dinosaurs?"
"No," said Little Panda.
"Well, count dinosaurs. And you know
there are lots of different kinds. Make sure
you count all of them. AND GO TO SLEEP!"

Little Panda started to count dinosaurs.
"Two hundred and two diplodocuses. Two
hundred and three diplodocuses. Two hundred
and four diplodocuses. Forty-six stegosauruses.
Forty-seven stegosauruses ... "

But still Little Panda couldn't sleep.
"Two zillion pterodactyls. Two zillion and one
pterodactyls. Two zillion and... Dad!"

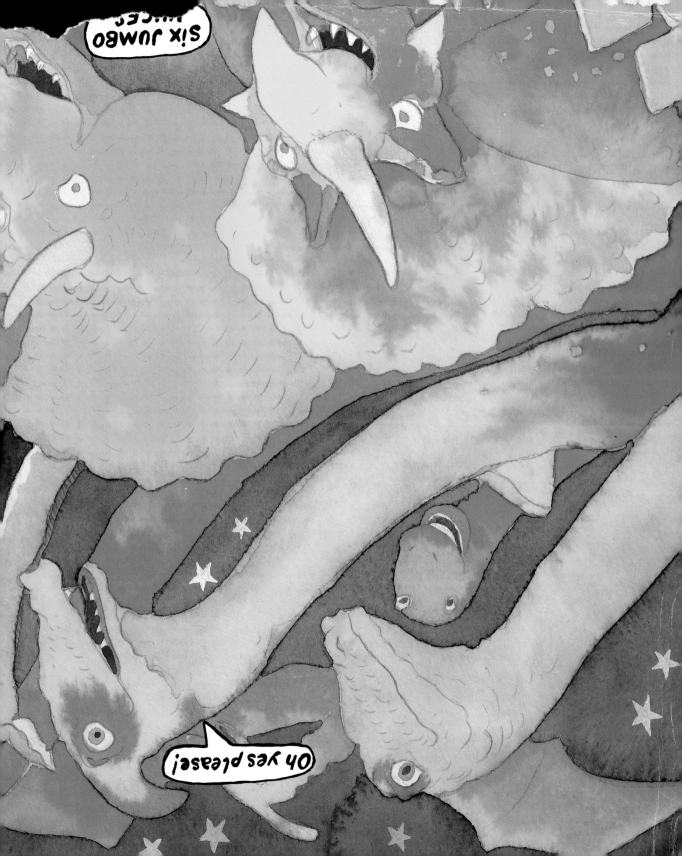

"Dad!"
"What is it now?" yelled Dad, as he threw the laundry at the cat and stomped up the stairs.

He pushed open Little
Panda's door.

Now lift the page...